Cat Essence

A Glimpse into the Feline Soul

By: Rikki, Tink, Mookie, Molly, Maggie, Bugger, Laura, and Robert Mayer

Mayer, Laura J.
Cat Essence: A Glimpse into the Feline Soul — 1st ed.
ISBN-13: 978-0-578-01757-0

Book design by Diana LeRoi-Schmidt
Photography by Laura and Bob Mayer
www.catessence.com

Dedication

To Rikki, most beloved gray ghost
To the infinitely wise Mao Tse Tink
To Mookie, a study of committed indifference
To Molly, the changeling
To Maggie, the little ocelot
To Bugger, my little narcissist

My husband and I coexist joyfully and peacefully with 4 cats. Each of our cats was a stray which being the cat lovers that we are, were adopted at various phases in our lives (and theirs).

To say we love cats is an ironclad cliché. It goes well beyond that. There are cat people and cat owners, and they are not the same. I wake up each morning with at least 3 cats on my bed. They know my routine and I know theirs. Going downstairs for coffee and various feline diets, we form a furry and human community. One jumps up on the sink for her water, since she disdains bowls on the floor. Mookie clamors to be let outside, regardless of the temperature. Rikki dominates the food bowl, and dares anyone else to come within a foot of her. Maggie and Molly, the youngest two, entreat us for food and attention with the same yearning of baby birds in the nest.

We believe in the essence and wisdom of cats, and hope that this book will convey that wisdom to you.

TABLE OF CONTENTS

TINKER: OUR EYES

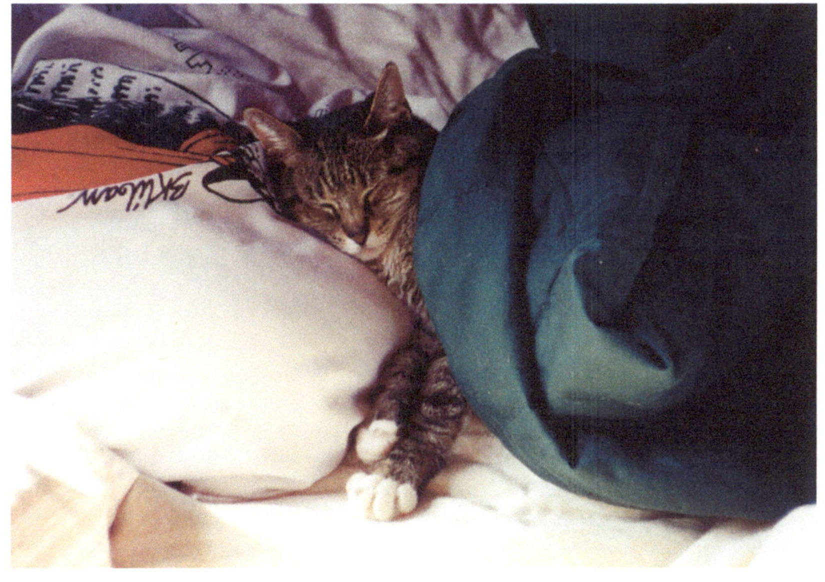

When you scrutinize our eyes while we are in your lap, you seem to want to want to prove the adage that the eyes are the windows to the soul. Not in our case. Your eyes are the windows to your soul. Ours are a screen that conceals our soul. Never try to look a cat in the eye. It doesn't frighten us; it's simply that a cat's soul is elusive. Our eyes do not weep or gleam with mirth. We understand things you do not. Cats, like human psychics, commune regularly with spirits. Cat's eyes and ears are attuned to a keen frequency beyond most human's capability.

So few of you notice the changes in our pupils. Your logical self writes this off to light adjustment. In truth, our eyes are tied to the tides and the pull of the moon. Our pupil adjustment is directly linked to the sun and the spirit of Mother Earth.

Eye contact between cats is about redemption and readiness. It is unquestioned allegiance to the message therein. Our eyes compel us to look and listen. So listen...

Tinker: We Already Know

So often, you turn to us with your desires, your complaints, your longing. You speak to us as though we were intelligent beings, which we are, yet your speech is condescending. So listen: we already know. We already know that sometimes you are trapped in a prison of your own making, that of your mind and ego. We already know that your rationale and emotions take over your freedom. We already know that perception in your world can make or break you. We already know, too, that there is no need for the endless manipulations you load on yourself and others. We know the truth about freedom. We know that security is an illusion, and we wonder at your futility in trying to obtain it. We know that community is about unconditional acceptance, and wonder at your relationship foibles.

It is no wonder to us that research has demonstrated the added longevity and sense of peace for people with pets (cats preferably).

After Bob's divorce, he was a wreck. He ran himself into the ground with work, drank too much, and played not at all. I tried to tell him, but he wasn't able to listen. He was too wrapped up in the myriad of senseless things you humans do to yourself, like guilt and shame and resentment and fear. Have you ever seen a cat ashamed?

I tried to tell him that spring does follow winter, that torrential rains lead to fertile ground, that darkness yields to sunlight. Even though we miss Bob and Laura when they are traveling, we know they'll come home. We know that our coat thickens at the onset of winter, and sheds in springtime. We know that living without change is death, and we embrace the opportunity to explore new places, sniff every morsel, and play new games. We listen when you pour out your woes, but we already know. Why don't you?

MOLLY: WE HATE KISSES

You humans have a penchant for kissing. Clearly, with the lips God gave you, this is perfectly normal for your species. However, we are clothed with fur and have no need or desire for your lips. Stroking is another matter altogether. Those of you who wear fur coats (and Thank God, Laura is not one of them) relish running your fingers through the plush fabric. But you may notice that you seldom kiss your ill-gotten coat.

We are no different. Being stroked is our equivalent to your being kissed. And while we will tolerate your lip nuzzling, you'll notice we don't stand for it very long. Get the picture?

TINKER: THE QUAKER CAT

Here's a cat lesson for you. Laura was watching Bugger face off with an unknown cat yesterday. Bug is too young and inexperienced to know yet when to fight, so he's clueless when he comes upon a feline outside of his immediate experience. Mostly, it scares the daylights out of him. Here's what happens when Bug is in the fight or flight mode. His orange tail swells to three times its normal size, and his heart pumps so wildly that you can see the entire side of his body throbbing. If he kept on in that mode for very long, he would die of a heart attack from sheer duress. Personally, that wouldn't faze me at all -- I think he's a spoiled brat, and he is a male. But the point is this, and it's one you humans never seem to get. You cannot continue to just sustain. Well, let me take that back for a moment. You can, but you are being untrue to yourself and to God if you do.

You cannot sustain hatred.
You cannot sustain peace.
You cannot sustain hostility.
You cannot sustain joy.
You cannot sustain suspicion.
You cannot sustain trust.

Life is change. Life is learning, growth, dynamic. In time, Bugger will learn when fighting makes sense, and when sleeping is a better idea. But he already knows sustenance is never a sure bet. Myself, I'm a pacifist. I have fought fiercely to defend myself, and I have my share of battle scars. Now, however, I have the knowledge to walk away from potential cat fights without any loss of pride or dignity. One day, Bugger will do the same. Will you?

Bugger: Language

I speak for the entire feline population and animal kingdom when expressing gratitude for not speaking your words (by the way, they don't call it the animal KINGDOM for nothing). Real communication has nothing to do with words, but you even muck that up by calling it "non-verbal" communication. A meow is worth several thousand of your dictionaries. It's pretty nutty to see you give so much power to words.

Listen, language is only listening and responding. It's just that simple. If the hawks cry danger, seek shelter. If the garden gate creaks open, seek and devour the fresh catnip. When the lid comes off the food bowl, eat. When the people leave the house, sleep. When they broadcast love, snuggle. I've yet to encounter a situation that couldn't be handled by a hiss, howl, meow, or purr.

Above all, silence is golden. You use this as an empty platitude, but fail to recognize the sacredness of the statement. Silence lets the light in. Silence soothes and heals. You can't be a stalker without being silent, and what's the point of living if you can't stalk?

RIKKI: CLEANSING

Cleanliness is next to godliness, but there's more to it than that. Cleaning is a never-ending process, but by no means neutral or insignificant.

Whenever Bob or Laura takes a shower or bath, I'm there on the bath mat. I listen and watch to see if they have cleansing experiences. They have, but both are as yet unaware of the mystery of cleaning.

For most of you humans, washing is a necessary and benign process, lumped in with eating and sleeping. We know better. Cleansing is often a painful and somewhat brutal thing. We use not just our tongues, but also our teeth to ferret out foreign substances from our skin. We clean with fierce and unwavering concentration because of cleaning's reward. Cleansing is exorcism from demons. Cleansing leads to restful fatigue. Cleansing results in being born anew, given a fresh start, a clean slate.

I'm very vocal when I clean. Much of this comes with age. I snarl ferociously during my bath. I pull out unwanted fur to get to my real skin underneath. Sometimes cats and humans require surgery to clean out the unwanted tumor. The cutting, the scarring, and the healing are all part of the cleansing miracle.

If a cat has ever licked you, you know that our tongues are like sandpaper. Not smooth and comforting, but rough and grating. To remove dead skin cells from your body, you need roughness. You need to scour and rub and dig deep to renew your skin. Scouring strips and uncovers the old to reveal the wonder of the new. Try to understand that the mystery of cleansing lies in the mental and spiritual realm, not the physical.

MOOKIE: ON CURIOSITY

Whoever said curiosity kills the cat? Curiosity certainly does not kill us; curiosity sustains us. We have an innate sense of exploration, and newness is essential to our nature. When the living room is littered with Christmas wrapping paper, decorations, and ribbon, we seek it out avidly. We chew the ribbon to ascertain its texture and determine if it is a feasible play toy. We roll ornaments across the floor to discover their velocity and durability.

I love the attic. It's got all kinds of cubbyholes and cracks and crevices. I've made a killing on mice up there. When we're outside, the chicken coop is the destination of choice for the same reason. Here's the rationale for good curiosity: Being curious leads one to explore. Exploration leads to discovery. Discovery leads to growth and that, my fur-less creatures, is what it's all about.

Most of you humans would like nothing better than to follow your curious instincts. You're just too frightened. You equate curiosity with the UNKNOWN—oooohhhhh... Get with the program—you don't know much anyway, so who cares if you poke and prod around in new things? And stop caring what anyone thinks of your behavior, because you're just not that important...*we are*.

Rikki: On Aging

I'm the eldest of the Mayer cats, going on 18. I probably have a few years left in me, but arthritis is already slowing my movements, and I spend most of my time sleeping. Sleeping is one of my favorite pastimes, so that doesn't bother me much.

Bob understands the implications of my age. He pays extra attention to me, and has told me periodically how much he'll miss me. Laura is in denial. She thinks I'll be around forever. She's not being ignorant, just loving. When 2 creatures live together as long as Laura and I have, they do tend to know each other thoroughly. She's rescued me from raccoon traps, treetops, and cat fights. She was there when I had both my litters. She and I have moved together 10 times. It's no wonder she thinks I'm invincible.

I don't mind aging. I was an only cat for 15 years, and was pretty pissed off when all of a sudden I was one of five. If anything, though, my sisters have given me more energy. My modus operandi is to be a surly, obstinate, unapproachable bitch. It works with Maggie and Molly, because they're too young to see through it. To keep Tinker and Mookie at bay, I've got to work harder. I chase them every chance I get and sometimes stand guard outside the door to the litter box to dare them to take a piss. Mookie gets intimidated very easily, which I love.

Getting old is easier with them. It's the same with you people. Is there any experience more desolating than dying alone? These guys will miss me when I'm gone, but they'll be with me when I'm going.

Rikki: On Aging

One final thought. At least you are more humane with us than your own species. When it's my time to go, Bob & Laura will have me put to sleep. There is no need for a Kevorkian cat. You let your own species lie like shells when all mental and bodily functions are gone because of your silly belief in living at all costs. Living is by far the greatest gift God bestowed on all creation. But death is its own reward, as it leads to yet another life – preferably as a feline.

Mookie: On Demands

You know that we are creatures of desire, and like many of you, become obstinate when any desire is thwarted. I'm probably the most vocal of the five of us when it comes to expressing what I want. Here's where I'm coming from with that: how will Bob and Laura know what I want unless I demand it? Unless you are gifted with psychic powers (and we know these powers exist, as we possess them), none of your species knows what you want.

When I get restless and it's too cold to go outside, I sit at the door to the attic and vocalize my desire until Laura relents and opens the door. She's learned that my persistence outweighs her patience by a huge margin.

The others make known their desires -- all cats do. When Molly wants on the porch, she gets up on her hind legs and paws at the pane with unwavering concentration. Tinker is so expressive that she only needs to direct a look at Bob or Laura to get her desires met. Maggie never knows what she wants, so she's not an issue.

Anyway, the point is, you might as well say what you want, and get what you want. You want it, so what's the point of keeping it to yourself?

Tinker: On Narcissism

Richard Bach said it well in his little book, Illusions: "Your conscience is the measure of the honesty of your selfishness. Listen to it carefully." We are all narcissists, cats and humans alike. We cats are just more ready to admit it. Selfishness is in our very nature. If I can drink fresh water from the sink faucet, why on earth should I condescend to lap out of a bowl on the floor?

Laura's a confirmed narcissist. She loves simple pleasures, including sleeping late, hot baths, a glass of wine with a good book, and curling up in front of a fire. She loves drinking hot chocolate and eating popcorn, and taking walks in the snow to see where the deer tread at night. Getting fired from that awful company awakened her, and we are gratified. People want what cats have, but they rarely allow themselves to gaze into that still pond and reflect on their own beauty.

Let yourselves be free to languish and indulge. You'll free your soul, I promise.

Molly: Dreaming

Sleep is essential to cats and humans. All these so-called guidelines you inflict on yourselves are crazy. There's no such thing as too much sleep. Look at the frequency with which babies nap. Who says naps are reserved for the young and old?

This is primarily because of dreams. Dreams are as integral a part of reality as reality itself, if not more so. Dreams guide us, teach us, warn us, and grow us. You view slumber as something totally passive and inactive, but it is quite the contrary. Laura understands this. She can easily sleep 8 to 10 hours a night, and would if she didn't have to work occasionally.

We treat our bodies like the treasures they are. We relish waking up on warm, thick comforters, pillows, and blankets. Slumber is a gift. It nourishes us, refreshes us, and soothes us. So then why, with your frantic life styles, do you continue to deprive yourself of life's best medicine, not just the renewal but also the illumination?

MOOKIE: ON TIME

Probably the most fallible foibles you creatures cling to are clocks and calendars. You've been led to believe there is such a thing called time, but there is no such thing. If ever you've been duped by an illusion, the compartmentalism of time is the BIG one. You can no more segment, slice and dice time than you can emotion. James Taylor sang "the secret of life is enjoying the passage of time." He didn't sing the secret of life is enjoying the passage of minutes, hours, seconds, or days.

I'm only telling you this because of what you allow your so-called "time" to do to you. Damn, people, it's painful to watch. You're too late, you're too early, you've got "time to kill" (oh, yeah, there's a good one). You've got no time, time is running out, the clock is ticking, a deadline is approaching -- is it any wonder you need so many drugs for stress?

You allow time to dictate your lives. We felines coexist with time. We are part and parcel of time, as it is us. We share with time the rising and setting of the sun and the advent of the moons. Laura's insomnia is a case in point. She is supposed to sleep through the night. Who says? You sleep when your body demands and needs it; and when you wake, you simply enjoy the passage of time.

BOB: ON CAT LOVERS AND CAT HATERS

There are cat lovers and cat haters, no in-between. You won't find oscillation in affection with the cat haters. When I was a cat owner, I used to wonder why anyone could hate a cat. In listening to the cats that live with us, I understood the answer.

Typically, people who hate cats love dogs. Ironically, cat lovers also tend to be dog lovers. What's wrong with this picture? Dog owners are obeyed religiously. Dogs provide their owners with immediate gratification. Dog owners are assured constantly of their dog's desperate need for them.

Cat owners, on the other hand, expect no response.   Cats are like gardens. Once you've tilled the soil, you plant in well-ordered rows. You water and fertilize the soil, and then you wait. Patiently. Your reward comes over time. Potato leaves greet you within days. Leeks demand that you wait months. Asparagus is not yours to enjoy until a full year goes by.

So it is with cats. Love from cats demands patience, attention, watering, and fertilizing. It was a full two years before Maggie would jump up on my chair, and three before I could pick up Molly. In time, we reap our harvest. Only in time.

Mookie: Blended Families

What a great time we had coming together with Rikki, Maggie, and Molly. The excitement was awesome! When Bob first brought me back from Cape Cod, Tinker hated me. We get very used to being an only cat -- the spoils are immense. No one else vies for the finished ice cream dish or gets to share in the crab meat & shrimp dinner. The litter box is for you and you alone. The bed is uncluttered but for one human. I learned all this after Bob brought me home. I was a stray when I lived on the Cape, and made my living out of garbage cans. I still love rummaging through garbage.

Anyway, Tinker was pissed and used to thrash me every time she got. I'm bigger than she is, but she's one tough cat. As soon as one of our fights would break out, Bob would throw a cushion at us and roar. Then it got to be a game to see how many times he would throw cushions. In the morning, they'd be all over the floor.

Tinker and me eventually made our peace. I'm a good fighter, but she can still thrash me, so I keep my distance. We really sided up when the other 3 arrived on the scene. What a trip! Bob put chicken wire the entire length of the door separating the upstairs from the down, and kept Tinker and me upstairs. When Laura brought in Rikki, Maggie, and Molly, it was pure mayhem. Rikki and Tinker went at it through the chicken wire!! Maggie and Molly disappeared into thin air -- those two had a rough time growing up in a woodpile, and they are skitterish.

So here you've got 5 of us in a relatively small house, and Bob and Laura gave up sleeping for a few days. Whether they were having dinner, watching TV, or going to sleep, the sound of hissing and growling was pre-imminent.

MOOKIE: BLENDED FAMILIES

Suffice it to say we made our peace. The chicken wire came down after 2 days and although there were a few fur-flying episodes, things quieted down. Rikki and Tinker act like they hate each other, but they've got a special bond. They know what it is to be the only cat. Rikki and I act like we hate each other, but it's because we love to taunt each other. We understand one another. She also grew up in the wild, and knows what it means to scrap for a living.   Maggie and Molly are inseparable, but that Molly is a troublemaker.

Fortunately, the farmhouse is a lot bigger than the log cabin, so there's plenty of room for us all. Occasionally, we'll scrap with each other, but there's no lasting animosity. All in all, it's an awesome family.

Scott Peck wrote a book called "The Different Drum". Laura went to a community-building workshop six years ago, and after experiencing genuine community, never forgot it. This is one reason she understands us so well. Peck talks about the four stages of community: peudo-community, chaos, emptiness, and community. You people are so bent on being seen a certain way you rarely get past the pseudo stuff. Cats, on the other hand, cut right to the chase. We go straight for the chaos because we want to get to the community, and you can't get there without that first step. How simple is that? Why you have such a fear of chaos is dumb.

Yes, we are territorial. But that does not prohibit us from community. Isn't it funny how you people can call us fiercely independent and truly territorial? Have you looked in the mirror lately?? You draw more lines in the sand than we would ever waste time with. Trust me, you might witness a black cat and a white cat entangled in battle, but I can guarantee you it isn't over the color of their fur.

Maggie: The Dance of Indecision

Life is choice. Every second of every minute of every day, choices are made by the human and animal kingdom alike. You tend to think that we are driven only by basic, primal instincts, by Abraham Maslow's lowest rung on the hierarchy, that of mere and brute physiological survival. The feline hierarchy is different, and one that humans would do well to adapt.

Physiological: We're with you on this one. Our physical needs, like yours are basic and in the forefront of our being.

Safety: No, here's where we digress. Safety and security are an illusion. Any cat out after dark knows this. Helen Keller said it best: "Security is mostly a superstition. It does not exist in nature, nor do the children of men as a whole experience it. Avoiding danger is no safer in the long run than outright exposure. Life is either a daring adventure, or nothing."

Belongingness and Love: We are in agreement on this, but we call it something else. It's really about freedom. It is about giving and receiving affection, but more so about that precious, misunderstood and unalienable right to be free. Free to alienate, free to attack, free to languish, and free to play. These are listed fourth in Maslow's hierarchy under esteem needs, but they belong here. How can you put freedom after belongingness and love, when belongingness and love cannot be accomplished without freedom? Go figure.

The other piece of esteem needs is this bit about having prestige and being well thought of. Like we care what you think! Take responsibility for yourselves and get over it.

So you see, the cat hierarchy is really only 2 tiers, as opposed to your five. There are the physical needs, and then there's freedom. Believe me, you've never met a cat that is not self-actualized. We have our peak experiences in being.

MAGGIE: THE DANCE OF INDECISION

You humans were taught mistakenly, and foolishly believed, that desire is taboo. What nonsense! This is as antithetical to your own nature as it is God's innate desire for you. Why do you persist in believing that His will differs so markedly from your own? What do you think He wants for you?

We choose whether to sleep, eat, play, explore, nap, run or fight. This is what most humans miss about choice -- every choice made is based on desire. You struggle so much with choice because you so consistently deny your desires. I assure you, no cat would every place desire in peril of denial.

The dance of indecision is nothing more than a conflict between choice and desire. The screened-in porch at our house provides a welcome relief from winter cabin fever. Even in the coldest weather, we remain constantly at the kitchen door until we are allowed out. I usually last all of 3 seconds outside. It's not the cold -- the outdoors is vast and mysterious, and a treasure for us. I choose this treasure consistently. But as soon as I get out, I need immediate reassurance that the warm kitchen is still available, and the love and constancy of Bob & Laura. So I plead to be let in again.

It's a dance, all right. Bob complains repeatedly about our fickleness. But each of our choices is based on our ever-changing desires, and those are ignored at our peril.

Maggie: Home

I speak for us all when talking about the farmhouse. Glenda was so right when she instructed Dorothy to repeat, "there's no place like home." There isn't. There's an old comforter at the top of the stairs tucked into the corner. Molly and Tinker monopolize this alternately. The round bed in the living room is for Molly alone — no one else wants it. The second bedroom upstairs is usually reserved for Tinker. I hang out with Rikki on Bob and Laura's bed, when Rikki isn't curled up in the computer room.

Bob and Laura do a check every night to make sure we're all in. We think it's a riot, but when Bob makes the rounds upstairs, we dutifully raise our heads to let him know we're present and accounted for. Then he and Laura yell up and down the stairs who they've located.

It's funny how people think that someday when we are outside we will not return. Robert Frost wrote such a great line — "Home is the place where, when you have to go there, They have to take you in." It speaks of unconditional love and obligation, which are not the polarities they appear to be. We will always come back to the farmhouse because of the love. Felines who are merely tolerated by their "owners" will always return home because they understand the pull of human obligation. Since we're going to be cared for either out of unconditional love or obligation, you might as well make it love. Trust me, it's so much easier.

Mookie: The Sixth Sense

Okay, picture this: You are walking down a dark alley in a large metropolitan city in order to take a short cut. You sense danger in the shadows, although the lighting is too dim for making out images. You have only ventured a third of the way down the alley, and the bright lights of the main thoroughfare are beckoning from behind. What do you do?

A cat would flee. A cat would sense the danger prior to even entering the alley. We do not rely on logic. Logic is vastly overrated and is more a hindrance to you than you comprehend. You humans are imprisoned by your so-called 5 senses. The Sixth through the Thirteenth are available for the taking -- why do you blindly imprison your mind? The Sixth sense precludes all others. Taste, touch, and smell of the mouse follow the kill. Sixth lets you know where the mouse is cowering. Sixth even precedes sight and hearing. On the darkest of nights and the brightest of days, we rely on Sixth. Think less; trust your gut. Leave me alone now.

Bob: Gluttons for Affection

These cats are always trolling for affection. Tinker has been the sole owner of my chest ever since I brought her home. When Laura is traveling, the routine is predictable. My first stop when I get home is the kitchen, where I turn on the obligatory tap for Tinker. While fixing dinner, the felines clamber for scraps of whatever I provide, although their preferences are vastly different. When I settle down in front of the television with a glass of wine, Tinker and Rikki alternately claim my body. Having been the sole proprietor for so long, Tinker gets really pissed off when Rikki does her famous wind-up and leaps into my lap. She usually jumps up on the arm of the chair, and alternately reproaches Rikki and me. Mookie, who is desperately intimidated and disliked by Rikki, makes her visits to the arm of the chair remarkably brief. Maggie and Molly are as yet not voluntary lap cats. Maggie loves affection, but only on her terms. Molly is willing to be picked up and responds with ardor to being stroked and held, especially for Laura when she's wearing her goose-down robe.

They are relentlessly demanding when it comes to love. They make claims on us that exasperate me to no end sometimes. Laura and I don't have children, but we still commiserate with parents.

We all want love on our own terms, and yet, our terms are often untenable. Best to be like cats – strictly ourselves – and give and return love as we feel so moved. Laura used to get so mad at me when we first got back together. We talked long and hard about the relationships we'd been in during our years apart. My favorite theme at the time was how important it was to work at a relationship. She scoffed at that ferociously. Labor and love were complete opposites for her, and she proved it. I have to admit, loving her is like loving the cats – requited, fulfilling, often frustrating, definitely exasperating, and always just plain fun.

Maggie: On Trauma

Laura did a bad thing to me one Christmas day. She wanted to show me off to Mom and Dad and Carol. It's only natural. Bob and Laura love us to pieces and they want to share us with everyone. But I am completely paranoid around any human other than Laura or Bob. Molly and I were both feral when we came to Laura. We were born in a woodpile, and the terrors of the night as kittens left us wary and suspicious. When I was captured, it was a struggle. You have to imagine a creature 50 times your size reaching down to trap and grab you. There's no time to determine good intentions. It's either fight or flight. You humans have the same aversion we do to new surroundings. You know how difficult it is to get used to the sounds and smells of new houses, and the awkwardness of meeting new people.

So here's what happened. Laura chased me out from under the bed where I was hiding, and trapped me against the wall when I tried to escape. I was twisting and writhing when she brought me downstairs, and the viewing of me didn't last long. It took hours of coaxing and coddling to get me downstairs after everyone left.

But here's the thing. I was over it the next day. That's one of the essential differences between cats and humans. We remember traumatic experiences, as do you. However, the remembrance only occurs when a similar experience is reenacted. Then it's over. You humans carry your trauma well into the future, which limits your ability to fully live in the present. You keep trauma alive in the form of fear that it will come alive in the future. What a waste of time! Sure, bad things will happen, but good ones will, too. Laura won't do that to me ever again, I know.

Maggie: On Trauma

When Laura first brought Molly home to her house in New Jersey, Molly hid in the basement and prayed for release back into the woodpile. She and Bob couldn't touch her, let alone find her. Things only got better when Laura brought me home. As sisters, we were lifelines to each other. We were totally freaked out by Rikki – what a monster!

When Laura's family starts the manipulation game on her periodically, she relives her trauma. But she's also learned, as we did long ago, that we have a choice when it comes to our memories. We can create a treasure chest or a Pandora's box. When we sleep and when we wake, we choose the realm of the treasure chest, those things that make us peaceful and content. You, on the other hand, store your memories, both good and bad, in a box you fear to open. Do not despair – even the miserable memories yield a blessing.

MOLLY: ON RENOVATION

Bob and Laura started renovation on the farmhouse in December 2000. What a lot of work and what a lot of dirt. First, they shut us up in the attic while the new heating system went in. It's a large finished attic, but 5 of us together for 8 hours made us all pretty testy. The only saving grace were the holes in the floor where the cast iron radiators were. These made for awesome mousing.

After a few months, getting shut upstairs while the kitchen renovation began was routine. Despite the long duration of this particular undertaking, we knew it was only temporary, and we cats are nothing if not totally adaptable. Consoling Bob and Laura was a full time job, though, at the end of each day. Why you people think you have control over anything is pure foolishness. As I tap this message out, the electricians have staged a "no-show" for 4 consecutive days. First Bob, then Laura, have stormed and cursed and cried over the delay. Get it clear, people: You have no control.

I'm now going to curl up against the cast iron baseboard in the spare room and go to sleep. This new heating system is the best.

Laura: The Pied Piper of Pine Tree Hill

When I wake each morning, I reach for the cat or cats in the bed, stroke them, and whisper my good mornings to their vocal and contented purring. On the landing, I stop to scratch Mookie's ears. Downstairs, in the kitchen, everyone appears simultaneously, and the morning feeding begins. Trust me, I'm not arrogant enough to believe that I have the power to lead these cats where they will. Yet, it's a fascinating and precious experience. Cats seduce us and we seduce them. We are at their bidding, and they are at ours.

At the end of the day, I stroll outside to conduct an exercise in futility -- the roll call. Well aware that Bug and Mook are scant meters away from my voice, I plead and cajole for them to come inside, knowing full well that I'm being peacefully watched and placidly ignored.

We speak of cats as being independent, but independence is too tame a word for the feline brand of freedom. Cats are confident trail blazers, prepared for danger, secure in strife, attuned to need, and free to wander and wonder.

Everyone eventually comes in at dusk, at a time of their own choosing. And I persist in my futile sunset exercise for my own selfish reasons. Sometimes, in the still of the evening, I feel the whispering of that watching cat.

Molly: Diet

If you took us all out for dinner, here's what the menu selections would look like:

Rikki -- cat food
Tinker -- pasta
Mookie -- chicken
Maggie & Molly -- shrimp and sushi
Bug -- only Laura's homemade raw diet

Bob is an ice fisherman. He's taught Laura how to handle polar tip-ups and how to jig for white perch. They have a blast, but the fun starts for me when they get home. What a treat the belly meat from a raw fish is!! Bob usually does all the cleaning, but when they came home with over 3 dozen fish, Laura finally consented to learn how to clean a fish. Naturally, she cleans 1 to his 4, but she's learning. The agonizing part for me is to have to wait for my belly meat. First of all, Laura refuses to cut into the fish unless it's dead. Bob showed her how to whack the fish on the head with the pliers. To be fair, she tried it, but just couldn't bring herself to really whack it (Bob calls it a love tap).

Bob scrapes off each and every morsel of the belly meat that comes with the skin, and oh, how we feast. Maggie and I are usually fighting over it. Fortunately, we don't have to contend with Tinker or Mook, but unfortunately, Rikki likes a taste occasionally. It doesn't present much of a problem, though, since she gums it to death before she eats it.

Don't deny us the pleasure of your foods, and for heaven's sake, read the ingredients on the canned crap you do expect us to relish.

MOOKIE: ON MOTHER EARTH

Many of you believe that cats should be kept indoors. Yes, there is the risk of feline leukemia, and yes, passing cars are perilous. But to keep us indoors is to deny a natural need and a God-given gift. Yes, we love warm blankets, and bowls of food and water, and toasty kitchens as much as people do. We also adore what our Creator has provided – glorious sun, tall grass, spring water, and tree bark. Why do so many of you persist in treating us like prisoners? Your own selfishness is no substitute for our need to be free. We already know and have explained to you that security is the most futile of illusions. You would not willingly shut yourself up within four walls for a lifetime, so why do it to us?

Let us have our earth before you destroy it. Pine Tree Hill is our haven, our home, our heaven, and our habitat. Laura may watch the younger ones like a mother hen, but Tinker and I have free rein. This disturbs Bob, because Tink crosses the street routinely, but he misses the point. We are in no more danger outdoors than you are, and probably less so since we are a smaller target.

We do not see boundaries as you do, and there are no property lines. There is only Mother Earth beckoning, inviting, cajoling, and singing. There are black snakes to pursue, a vegetable garden to peruse, a pond to investigate, owls to ponder, deer to chase, mice to kill, and chipmunks to race. There are trees to conquer, fields to run wild in, stonewalls to leap, and above all, freedom from shelter and the four walls of restriction.

Tinker: We Already Knew

Whenever Laura returned home from a business trip, Rikki would meet her in the kitchen with a plaintive sound of displeasure. None of us are happy when Bob and Laura go away, but Rikki really pined when Laura was away. It's not that Bob didn't smother her with attention. It's just that she and Laura had an intense bond, which was a mixture of love and mutual torment. Laura could roll Rikki on her back and nuzzle her belly, whereas most people got paw whacked just for petting Rikki.

Rikki was the epitome of polarity. She was the most demanding and the least demanding. She was the most affectionate and by far the surliest. She alternated as she pleased between being the most yielding of cats and the most obstinate. Perhaps she was such a powerful matriarch because she was the only one among us who experienced cat birth. Rikki's legacy was in her very expression of life -- pure, unadulterated, uncompromising, and non-negotiable. With Rikki, you got what you got.

As was her wont, Laura scooped Rikki up in her arms the minute she walked in the door from her trip. We all noticed her alarm, as Rikki was noticeably lighter in weight. That was the beginning of the end. The doctor prescribed appetite stimulants, and Bob and Laura tried desperately to get Rikki to eat. The only success they had was with tuna water. Rikki would lap up a few sips, and leave the tuna meat untouched. During the last week, Bob kept her alive with an IV.

Rikki was ready to go. We all knew it, and we knew that Bob and Laura would not see it. I've heard it said that animals live longer and healthier lives than people because animals have no memory. That's untrue. We remember poignantly. The difference between you and us is that we do not saturate ourselves in the past. Was it Confucius who said "Dwell not on your mistakes, and thus make them crimes?" Like thought, memory is a blessing, which you often choose to abuse.

When the decision and the appointment were finally made, I walked through the screen door and Rikki and I

TINKER: WE ALREADY KNEW

touched noses. This brought tears to Bob's eyes. Understandable, given that we had fought over territorial rights since our first day together. But I knew she was going and wanted to say good-bye. Rikki knew that I knew. She gladly passed the matriarchal wand on to me. This is a job that demands dignity, authority, and periodic ferocity. Rikki was incomparable in the role.

Life goes on. Bob and Laura will no doubt deal with each of our deaths and the subsequent pain. But they must see the reverence of Rikki's death, Rikki's peace, and our acknowledgement of her passing. The large blue pillow in the living room remains uninhabited, and will forever. She was dying from an incurable cancer, and was only waiting for Bob and Laura to send her on her way. Their suffering was visible, and their tears unstoppable. The rest of us? We already knew.

Bugger: Rules are, There Ain't No Rules

What a bunch of uptight females. When Rikki sent me, she told me I was joining a large family, but I never expected such prima donnas. Geez Louise. They can't take a joke and they don't even know how to play. Maggie's paranoid, and Tinker is a grouch. Molly is coming around – she at least likes to get into as much trouble as I do. Mookie will probably be a blast outside in the spring, but the only thing she does inside is terrify Maggie. No wonder Maggie's so paranoid.

What a cool place it is, though, especially with the renovation. These guys build something new every day, and I get to check it out when I'm released from the second floor. I got loose in the basement one day. Totally awesome! You could get lost in the crawl spaces down there. In the kitchen, there's this monster chimney at the center of the house. The guys are covering up one wall at a time, but you can still get between the wall and the original chimney. Tinker gets fed on the mantel, because she's got a bum kidney and is on a special diet. What I can do is cut through the tunnel between the wall and the chimney, and make a pass at her from behind. She's easily pissed off, so I get a lot of her food. She gets the canned stuff, so that's cool.

Bob's got everyone trained with his tone of voice. He has his own unique way of saying NOOOOO, and that stops the others in their tracks. Wimps. Like I really want to learn manners. Laura's a total rollover. I mean, she's fun and I like her, but she couldn't discipline a snail. She's too much of a softie. Which is good for me come spring. I'll be outside before you know it. For now, I'm outta here.

Laura: Finding Bugger

I couldn't stop crying after the vet gave Rikki the injection that stopped her heart. He gave her a tranquilizer first to relax her, and we spent ten minutes holding and stroking her. Oh, God, it broke my heart to hold that tiny gray head in the palm of my hand and look into those fatigue-driven green eyes. We took her home on her flannel-encased pillow and buried her by the pond under a mountain laurel. We wrapped her in Bob's well-worn wool sweater, her alternative bed when she wasn't on the blue pillow.

The house was so empty that day. Bob said it best. Our cats create an environment, a distinct climate in our home. Rikki was an environment unto herself.

The following morning, almost 24 hours since Rikki had died, I was cleaning the boat in the driveway. When I heard a cat's cry, I jumped down and found Tinker under the boat. After putting her back in the house, I returned to my cleaning. Further mews ensued. How do I describe my heartbeat when I looked under the forsythia and saw a little mite of an orange tabby? I ran for the house at breakneck speed and returned with a saucer of canned food and a plate of dry food. Food could not coax this kitten out of hiding. It wanted a chase. I followed the kitten to the end of the driveway, paralyzed when it crossed the street. When it disappeared into the woods, I followed on private property, praying that this kitten would be ours. When the cries of the kitten became too distant, I sat down in the driveway and wept. That's when it came running up to me, and got "snagged" as Bob and I say when we scoop up a cat in our arms.

Laura: Finding Bugger

I do not know where the Bugger came from. He is the first male cat we've ever owned, and he won a place in our hearts immediately. Neither of us was ready for another cat so soon after Rikki's death, but we are convinced he was a gift from Rikki. And what a gift!

Bugger earned his name from climbing the screens and walls to get to insects. Anything was game – wasps, ladybugs, moths, and ants. He is fearless with the girls. He is consumed with curiosity and unabashedly affectionate. He was crawling with fleas, and had severe conjunctivitis in one eye. I have no love of people who desert kittens, but I'm thankful to whoever dropped him off in our neighborhood. He has become an integral part of our family, a source of joy. The environment is different without Rikki. Her regal manners and haughty behavior provided wisdom, contemplation, and peace within our household. Bugger brings spontaneity, boundless energy, and chaos to the family. I've ceased to hang the lace curtains in the sitting room, knowing they'll only be pulled down within the hour.

He sleeps with us, as did Rikki. When we stir in the morning, he is immediately on his paws and inquiring with his motorcycle purr when we intend to get up. Like the other cats, he does not sleep on the blue pillow.

So we are once again, with no respite, a family of seven. Rikki died at age 20, and Bugger is not yet one year old. Rikki's death and Bugger's advent make us realize that life and death are truly intertwined. Rikki will never leave our hearts, and one day, when Bugger is ready to go, we have no doubt that the two of them will consort lovingly in the next life.

TINKER: NOCTURNAL HEALING

Laura had a particularly bad day recently. She received alarming news from her pulmonologist on her breathing. Even though she'd quit smoking, Bob still smoked and we slept with Bob and her every night. What can I say to people who profess to be allergic to us? Get over it. We shed no more of our fur than you do skin and hair, and at least we don't use perfume or cologne. I think you "allergic to cats" people are just looking for an excuse to be isolationist snobs. Frankly, we don't care. And even if Laura was desperately allergic to each of us, she would never let us go. That's love for you.

Anyway, she was pretty upset that night. Her lungs were shot, she had PMS, and the house was in its usual trashed state due to renovation. To top it off, a number of dirty dishes had accumulated, and she was less than overjoyed at scrubbing things out in the upstairs bathtub. Suffice it to say there were a lot of tears that night.

I could not help Laura with her insomnia that night. I could and did, however, give her peace of mind. Many, many people have told your kind about the spirit world and how those that pass on surround us in multitudes. In your fear and arrogance, most of you refute this. We felines, however, are spirit liaisons. As she lay weeping, I crept under the covers and lay beside her. While she stroked me, I emanated the peace coming from those kindred spirits. Her grandparents were there, as were her spirit mentors, King, Kennedy, and Cicero included.

It's a wonder you people don't understand this. When you visit the grave site of a loved one, you spend your time recalling and recollecting memories of life situations. What your loved ones would rather have you do is listen to them there and then. They have a different message for you now, but you remain stuck in their life. Haven't you yet learned that death is a new life?

You are a gifted species, but you don't know everything. You insist on keeping yourself separate from the earth, when you are an integral part of it. Trees and ponds on a rolling landscape are a natural sight for you, because you see trees and ponds belonging to land. What you fail to see is that you are as much a part of that land as the pond

Tinker: Nocturnal Healing

and the tree. You are not distinct from the sun that warms your skin, or the air your lungs breathe, or the ground you traverse. You are soil and water and earth, and people who have died try to tell you this.

Laura only knew that I crawled under the covers, and she rightly viewed my gesture as healing and consolation for her pain. She missed out on the universal healing given by those who have passed on.   I write this to teach her to listen.

Bob: Tinker

When I think of Tinker, her gentle leap of grace comes first to my mind. My chest was her rightful throne, and the kitchen faucet her personal fountain. If I slept too late for her satisfaction, a subtle paw would gently tap my eyelid.

I am not a member of any organized religion, but Tinker taught me a lot about God. She made her first appearance in my life as a young kitten sitting in a cardboard box at an office in Stamford. I was freshly raw from the end of a marriage, and was carrying on as best I could with my work. It's easiest to say that I found Tinker, but of course the reverse is true. A need was formed and filled. Rikki sent the Bug to ease our grief -- a need was formed and filled.

We refer to the deer, geese, skunks, raccoons, coyotes and other species we coexist with as wildlife. Fifty pound bags of sunflower seeds for the birds are no stranger to our porch or pocketbook. Each spring, the cracked corn comes out for Couscous and Miss Muse, the pair of geese who have adopted our pond. On the bitterest of winter days, Laura will core and scatter apples for the deer. We do these things out of choice and because we love the wildlife we see. The wildlife? They don't need it. Miss Muse eats corn out of Laura's hand, but she can and does subsist and thrive with or without the handout. Jesus said "Are not two sparrows sold for a penny? Yet not one of them will fall to the ground apart from the will of your Father." The biggest difference between us and wildlife is that they comprehend being in God's domain.

Like I said, I'm not into any organized religion, but I sometimes wonder how exactly we are different from the wildlife. You've got to respect how skillfully these creatures weather a New England winter none the worse for wear. And if you believe the words of Jesus, it begs an explanation of why we become so easily paranoid and paralyzed over green pieces of paper. Can we wildlife humans survive without money?

These are some of the questions put into my mind when staring into those infinitely wise hazel cat eyes. Laura

BOB: TINKER

didn't nickname her Mao Tse Tink for nothing.

She died in her sleep when we were on vacation in Cape Cod the summer of 2002. I am still heartbroken that I was not with her when she died, but I am comforted that she went in her sleep. We were not surprised to get the phone call. Tink's deterioration was rapid and we said prayerful good-byes to her prior to leaving the house that Saturday morning. We buried her next to Rikki, and our two beloved matriarchs who sustained us through so much grief watch over us. At our darkest moments, our eldest cats gave comfort that truly surpasses human understanding.

When I think of Tinker, her gentle leap of grace comes first to my mind, followed by a leap of faith that life is exactly as it should be.

BUGGER: LESSONS

I didn't write much of this book, because I have better things to do. But for my fellow brethren out there, listen up. Laura started us on this natural raw diet, and damn, is it good. Try to get a piece of that action.

My sisters have done all kinds of pontificating and preening like the prima donnas they are. I've got the last chapter, so listen up. Here's what you need to do:

1. Play hard. Play very hard. But don't hurt and don't get hurt.
2. Eat as much as you want, but try not to get as fat as Molly -- what a tank!
3. Excavate the litter box every time you use it -- this is way cool.
4. Sleep next to a person in such a way that they can't possibly turn over without disrupting you. Hee hee.
5. Run. It sets you free. But don't forget to come home.
6. Touch, taste, and smell everything that you are and everything you are not.
7. Don't forget to listen -- and teach these guys what you learn. Just don't expect they'll always get it.
8. Love your people. Just don't ever let on that you do.

One other thing. The answers really are blowing in the wind. Wind cools and fuels, wind rises and sinks. Wind roars and whispers, soothes and destroys. Wind reveals and obliterates, clears and obscures. Wind fuels and eliminates fire. Listen to its song. Every answer you seek, every chance you fear, every choice you desire, every paradox you know -- the answers are blowing in the wind.

9 780578 017570